CONTROLLED

THE ALTERNATIVE

CONTROLLED

PATRICK JONES

darbycreek
MINNEAPOLIS

Darby Creek
A division of Lerner Publishing Group, Inc.
241 First Avenue North
Minneapolis, MN 55401 U.S.A.

For updated reading levels and more information, look up this title at www.lernerbooks.com.

Cover and interior photographs © John Smith/Dreamstime.com (girls); © iStockphoto.com/joeygil (locker background).

Main body text set in Janson Text LT Std 12/17.
Typeface provided by Linotype AG.

Library of Congress Cataloging-in-Publication Data

Jones, Patrick, 1961–
        Controlled / by Patrick Jones.
        pages cm. — (The alternative)
        Summary: Rachel Kelly was prepared for a high-stress, over-scheduled junior year filled with AP classes, orchestra, and an unrequited crush but after her troubled cousin Misty moves in and upsets Rachel's controlled life, Rachel finds herself becoming sympathetic toward Misty.
        ISBN 978–1–4677–3902–3 (lib. bdg. : alk. paper)
        ISBN 978–1–4677–4635–9 (eBook)
        [1. Cousins—Fiction. 2. Conduct of life—Fiction. 3. High schools—Fiction. 4. Schools—Fiction. 5. Personality disorders—Fiction. 6. Family life—Fiction.] I. Title.
PZ7.J7242Con 2014
[Fic]—dc23   2013041391

Manufactured in the United States of America
1 – BP – 7/15/14

WITH THANKS TO ALLYSON, ANALEYSHA,
ARIANNA, BRITTNEY, KIARA, AND NAYALIE
SPECIAL THANKS TO SYDNEY BAIR, WHO
READ AN EARLIER VERSION OF THIS WORK.
-P.J.

1

"Rachel, we need to talk."

I'm barely through the front door, viola case still in hand. But my parents are blocking my path to my bedroom. I follow them into the kitchen.

"Rachel, honey, sit down." As always, I do as I'm told.

"I have some news about my sister," Dad says real soft. But the news doesn't form into words. Dad just sits there and stares at his hands.

Finally, Mom speaks for him. It's what she does best. "Your Aunt Molly died."

I'm not sure what I should pretend to feel. Surprise? Sadness? I've met Aunt Molly maybe twice. It's not like I actually knew her. And judging by the little that my parents have said about her, she wasn't worth knowing. But Dad is working his jaw and not making eye contact. That's code in our family for *I'm upset. I won't talk about it. But you should care.*

"Sorry, Dad," I say. No points for creativity. But what else do they expect? "How did it happen?" That's what I'm really feeling: curiosity, like a person driving past a car wreck.

"Does that matter?" His nonanswer is the answer. A drug overdose is my best guess.

"So, we have to go to the funeral?" I prompt. That wasn't how I was counting on spending my weekend. School starts next week, and I need to be ready. I don't have time to go all the way up to Hibbing and back.

He sighs. "The funeral will be here, in Woodbury. But it's not just that. Her daughter—your cousin, Misty—needs a place to live."

"Wait . . . what?" Every molecule in my body suddenly screams in fear.

"Your mom and I are going to pick her up tomorrow. She's moving in." I wish life had sound effects like a movie. I want thunder.

"Do I have to share my room?" I think of my closet. My bookshelf. The corner where I keep my viola case and my folders full of music. There's no space for another person.

"She'll stay in Denise's room. Denise doesn't need her own room here while she's across the country in grad school." Out East, overachieving, as always.

"But what about when Denise comes home at Thanksgiving?"

Dad sighs again. Why does he sound like he has asthma whenever I even hint at talking back? "We'll work something out," he says. "For now, the main thing is to be there for Misty."

"Honey, we expect your help on this," adds Mom.

"Misty will go to school with you. She's actually in the same grade as you." Even though she's a year and a half older? That sounds promising. Besides, don't kids like Misty go to alternative schools, like Rondo in St. Paul?

"I barely know Misty," I remind Dad. "You never wanted Aunt Molly around."

"She's still family," Dad says. "And she's only seventeen. She can't live on her own, and I won't let her go into foster care. She needs us."

"For how long?"

"At least until she graduates from high school, so this year and next," Dad says.

"Oh, you think she'll graduate?" I snap. Her mom was a dropout. That's one of the few things I know about her.

"I told her that's a condition of her living here." Mom now. "She's got to stay in school. Rachel, honey, you can help her. You're a straight-A student. You can set an example."

"Mom, seriously?" I've scheduled out my junior year, and this won't fit into it. Three AP classes, first-chair viola in orchestra, college visits in the spring, but not this.

"You can at least be a friend to her," Mom adds. "I'm sure she needs that right now. And I suspect her friends from home haven't been a good influence."

I can't believe this. My parents have always

made decisions for me, which is annoying but usually not worth a fight. But this is the first time they've picked a friend for me. That's a new low. "She's a stranger. You can't just *assign* her to me!"

"This is going to be hard on us all," Dad says. "We'll all have to adjust to the change."

I want to shout: *I like my school. I like my friends. I like my life. And I don't like change.*

"What happens if it doesn't work out?" I ask. When's the last time I asked that question? Third grade, maybe, when Mom told me I was going to learn to play viola?

"It will work out." Mom's eyelids flicker like hummingbirds. Just like mine do when I tell a lie.

2

"Do you have something I can wear to the funeral?" Misty asks. She picks at clothes in my closet, wreaking havoc on my system.

"I don't think we're the same size." I'm small, everywhere. She's big. Not fat but curvy. And we definitely don't share the same fashion sense. She's wearing a too-tight, long-sleeve gray tee, even in the August heat. The cheap bracelets covering both arms don't help.

"Maybe you could look in Denise's closet. I think she's a little closer to your size."

"Really?" Almost everything Misty says

sounds like she's surprised.

"You're taking her room, why not take her clothes?" I let myself get snide with her, the way I never do with my parents.

She steps away from my closet and I shut the door, fast.

"Could you help me get my stuff from the car?" she asks.

"Sure." I lead the way outside into a wave of heat.

"So what's Woodbury High like?"

I still think she should be in Rondo Alternative, but nobody asked my opinion. "Avoid jerks, you'll be fine," I answer.

"Everything at my old school sucked, except my friends," Misty says. "So much d-r-a-m-a. Hey, that's a sweet ride your dad's got. Could you drive me back up to Hibbing sometime to visit my friends?"

I look away. "You don't have a license?" I ask.

"I drove my mom lots of—" she starts/stops. "But I couldn't afford the driving class."

"Oh." I don't ask why she had to drive her mom. I don't want or need those details.

"You'll meet my friends soon. They all said they'd come down from the Iron Range to visit me."

Dad had left the trunk of the new Lexus unlocked. I pop it open. "Sounds good." Why do I lie to her? Nothing about that sounds good. I don't need to meet her friends. I already have Dana and Sarah.

When Denise moved to college, her belongings filled two cars. Grad school took a U-Haul. "You take two, and I'll take two," Misty says.

Misty, why do the contents of your life fit into four black trash bags? I think as I pull two overstuffed bags from the trunk.

We take trash bags into the house rather than out to the curb. I've entered a backwards world.

3

"Don't even think about it, Rachel."

Mom scolds me for reaching into the pocket of my black dress to check my phone. Dana just texted me about setting up an AP Chem study group.

"Be respectful," my mother hisses.

"Okay, Mom, relax." Like relaxing is something anyone in our family knows how to do.

I glance at my father. He's crying. He's the only one, but it is a small crowd. Just us four standing in the cemetery. I haven't seen Dad cry since Grandpa died. I haven't seen Mom cry since . . . ever? But she's holding Dad's hand. For her, that shows a world of feeling.

Today, it's Misty who wins the prize for giving away the least emotion. Her mom is in a wooden box about to go into the dirt, but Misty is stone-faced. "You okay?" I whisper to her as we wait for the minister to show up. She's wearing Denise's clothes—a black dress and, despite the blistering heat, a light sweater.

"Thanks for being here," Misty says, too loud for the setting.

"I'm sorry Mom wouldn't let me invite my friends Sarah and Dana to be here," I whisper.

"She wouldn't let my friends come from Hibbing either." She's so loud; does she know that? When Mom and Dad said no to friends, Misty threw a fit. Yelled. Cursed. But no tears. Just like now. "At least you're here."

"Of course I'm here. I'm family." I try to sound like I mean it. If I had to move three hours away from Dana and Sarah, I'd want someone to tell me a kind lie.

"No, you're more than that," she says. "You're the best friend I've got in two hundred miles."

The sun burns my skin. Misty's sad smile chills me. I wish Dana and Sarah were here.

A car door slams behind us. Finally, the minister. We turn. Then stare.

It's not just the minister. Three other men are walking this way too.

"What's he doing here?" Misty spits at my father.

Dad looks unsure of himself. Misty kicks the dirt with Denise's ill-fitting black shoe. "If he's here, I'm not!" Misty's voice is loud enough to raise the dead around us.

Dad reaches out for Misty's arm, but she's too fast, too strong, too angry. She runs for the car.

"Misty!" Mom yells.

"Let her go," Dad whispers.

The three men join us at the grave site. The man in the middle nods at my father. I peer at him out of the corner of my eye. Too-large blue suit. Short red hair. Unshaven face. Flat eyes.

"Dad, who is that?" I whisper.

Dad never looks up. "Misty's father."

The minister finally starts reading. Typical

valley of death stuff. Dad cries more. I should hug him, but I can't take my eyes off these three men.

The other two men don't wear suits. They're in uniforms. Shined black shoes. Tan shirts and slacks. Hats, which they've respectfully removed. The large man in the middle bows his head and raises his rough-looking hands for the prayer. Along with the minister's voice, I hear the same noise that caught our attention when the men first approached.

It's the rattling of the prison chains around Misty's father's wrists and ankles.

4

"Oh my God, Rach, who is that?" I have no idea why Misty keeps calling me "Rach."

"Colt Martin," I answer. Stupid me. If I stop answering to "Rach," maybe she'll stop saying it. "And his girlfriend, Shawna Reeves," I add.

"He is so hot!" Colt is one of the Woodbury's sun gods. I'm not even in his orbit. I pray Colt can't hear us from across the Kohl's store crowded with back-to-school shoppers.

"He's probably here just to spy in the girl's dressing rooms. He's a perv."

"Oh, but he is *fine*." Misty's face glows

despite, or maybe because of, the layers of makeup.

"Yeah, and he knows it. He's obsessed with himself."

"I can see why." She's almost panting.

"Remember when you asked about what Woodbury High was like? I said it's okay if you avoid jerks. And Colt is one of the biggest jerks."

"What did he do to you?"

I shrug. People like Colt don't even know I exist. Except when they need a target for a joke.

"Name one thing." Sometimes Misty gets the tone and glare of a school bully.

"Okay. For breast cancer awareness month, Colt offered free hands-on mammograms."

Why is Misty laughing? Laughing loud enough to draw attention. Probably even Colt's attention. I frown. "Both of Dana's grandmothers died of breast cancer. It's not funny."

Mom comes up the aisle toward us. "Girls, are we about ready?" She sounds exhausted.

"I didn't find anything." I can't shop with Mom. I need Sarah and Dana's fashion guidance.

"Misty, what about you?" Can Misty tell

from the tone that Mom is angry? Misty turns around with her shopping cart full of clothes. Mom's mouth twitches.

"We agreed on a certain amount of money." *Agreed* means Mom decides.

"I guess I got carried away, Mrs. Kelly. I can put it all back if you want me to."

I kept telling Misty she was getting too much stuff, but she just laughed. Now she's acting all humble—but also putting it on my mom, saying "if you want me to."

"No, but let's see what you really need." Mom starts looking through the clothes.

Misty pouts. "I need all of it."

Mom laughs. "I don't think you need these." She pulls a pair of red thong underwear from the cart.

"Yes, I do." Misty takes the underwear and puts it back in the cart. Right on top.

"I'm not paying for a seventeen-year-old girl to wear thong underwear," Mom says as I blush.

"Why not? You have the money. Why can't you spend some on me and not just on Rachel?" *Leave me out of it,* I think. Yet I can't help being a little impressed. Nobody ever questions Mom.

"I'll buy the other things," Mom says. "I just don't approve of this."

"Never mind!" Misty topples the cart. The clank of its metal frame hitting the floor echoes through the aisle. Clothes spill out in a tornado of color.

"Pick that up." Mom's voice doesn't change, of course. She would never yell in public.

"Or else?" Misty folds her arms under big breasts, almost pushing them in Mom's face.

"Or I'm not buying you any of this." Mom uses the stern voice that I've dreaded all my life.

Misty snorts. "Whatever, Karen, I'll just steal it later. And don't tell me what to do *ever* again."

For the first time I can remember, Mom is speechless. She stands there with her mouth open, like Misty stole her voice box.

I'm silent too. Not because I have nothing to say but because I don't dare let out the cheer that's building inside me. *Go, Misty, go!*

"Girls, we're leaving," Mom says. But it's pretty clear that Misty just arrived.

5

MISTY TO ME: "What's up, Rach?"

I sigh. After avoiding it since the day she moved in, I finally friended Misty, and now she's interrupting my life online as well as at home.

ME TO MISTY: "Nothing."

Why is she messaging me from the other room? Why does she keep calling me Rach?

I go back to chatting with Dana, Sarah, and—*sigh, heartbeat, sigh*—Kevin Liu.

MISTY TO ME: "What time do we roll from the crib for school?"

ME TO MISTY: "6:30." I have orchestra zero hour. I don't know her schedule.

I minimize Misty. I chew on a nail and ponder what to say next to Kevin. I type, erase, repeat, but don't hit Send.

"Rachel, honey, time for bed," Mom says from my doorway.

"Okay, Mom, I'm logging off." She heads toward the living room, where Misty is using the old desktop.

I take a quick look at Kevin's page. We've got three AP classes and orchestra together. He's the kind of person who always gets voted Most Likely to Succeed. Not to mention Most Likely to Steal Rachel Kelly's Heart.

"Misty, I said now," Mom says from the other room.

I look at Misty's page and her most recent adds. Sarah. Dana. When did she friend them? Why?

"I won't tell you again." Mom cranks it up another decibel. "That's it!" Two-decibel increase. Now defined as shouting. "Jack, get out here!"

My father stomps by my room. This is going to be a good one. I race for the door to listen.

"Misty, I told you. You need to be in your room and in bed by 11:00 on school nights."

"Why can't I have a computer in my room like Rachel?"

"Trust is earned."

"So you don't trust me!"

"Misty, honey, we barely know you." Mom reduces the volume. "Just calm down."

"Don't call me honey, Karen, and don't tell me to calm down!"

"Let's not wake the neighbors." Dad sometimes walks angrily or talks harshly, but like Mom, he rarely yells.

"Why? Don't you want them to know that someone like me is living in your house?"

"Misty, you're my niece and we want you here. I know this isn't easy, losing your—"

"I lost all my friends and you won't let me visit them or let them come here!"

"We want you to settle in here first, and then we'll visit your friends."

"I wish I could have lived with them instead of with you. You hate me!"

"Misty, we don't—" That's as far as Dad gets

before I hear something—a chair?—crash onto the floor.

"Okay, that's enough," Dad says. "Misty, please go to your room."

Misty slams against the walls and then pauses outside my door. "Enjoy the show, Rach?"

"Rachel, is that your cousin talking to Colt and Shawna and Daniel and Alix?" Dana asks, peering across the cafeteria.

I shrug and take a bite of salad. "I don't know, and I don't care."

"That's pretty harsh," Sarah says as she rearranges the carrot sticks in front of her by size.

"Misty's life is her business. I've got enough to think about without taking responsibility for her." It's the first day of school and I already feel behind. Orchestra practice in the mornings half the week and in the afternoons the other half, mountains of homework, ACTs coming up . . .

I start to ask Sarah about college visits, but Dana cuts me off. "Misty's coming this way."

Sarah and Dana quickly pull out their phones so they can avoid her. I'm not quick enough.

"Crowded in here, isn't it, Dana?" Misty sits down with her over-full tray.

"First lunch is the worst," Dana says without looking up from her phone.

"This pizza is the worst," Misty dips the sausage pizza in a bowl of ranch before taking a bite.

"We wouldn't know." I love the word *we*, meaning Sarah, Dana, and me.

"You don't eat pizza?" Misty chews too loud. "Any of you?"

Sarah points to her salad. "I'm a vegan. I don't eat any animal products."

"And I'm a vegetarian, like Rachel," Dana adds. "We'd be vegan if not for vegan cheese." Dana and I both pretend to put our fingers down our throat. Sarah rolls her eyes.

"But didn't I see you eat chicken this

weekend?" Misty asks. I want to kick her under the table.

"Okay, I'm a vege-hypocrite. I blame my mom. She's the contradiction queen."

"Like how?"

"Like she has a pro-environment license plate but drives that giant SUV."

"Do you think she'll let me drive it?" Misty asks. "I signed up for driver's ed through the school."

"You could ask her," I say. I want to add "And I know you will," but I *do do do* want to be nice.

"Hey, Dana, we match!" Misty says. She holds her wrist next to Dana's. Pink bracelets.

"Where'd you get that?" I ask. I make a mental note to check my dresser when I get home.

"Pink power!" is all she says. She keeps talking to Dana. "Are you doing the three-day?"

Okay, that's too much. How does she know that we walk the Komen breast cancer fund-raiser?

"Of course—do you want to join us?" Dana asks out of nowhere. "It's next weekend."

"Well, if I'm ungrounded by then." Misty glares at me like her grounding is my fault. "Hey, Sarah, can I see your phone?" She reaches across the table.

"I guess." Sarah looks worried and amused at the same time.

Misty holds the phone in her palm like a pearl. "I gotta get one of these. My phone has like zero memory."

While she stares at Sarah's phone, we stare at the ink covering the back of her hand. "Whose phone numbers are those?" asks Dana.

"Colt Martin's and Alix Hawkins's."

"You're kidding," gasps Sarah. "*Those two* want to hang out with you?" She and Dana start grilling Misty about how she managed it. Dana actually grabs Misty's hand to get a better look at the numbers.

But I'm not looking at the scribbled digits anymore. I'm looking at Misty's right arm where her sleeve has slipped. There's a spot just an inch above the wrist where Misty's skin is laced with lines of red scars.

7

I knock on the open door of Denise's room. Misty's room.

"What?" Attitude fills the word. Her back is still to me. Eyes on her phone.

"Um, are you okay?"

"I'm fine." Every time I shut my eyes I see those scars on her arms. Yet she says she's fine.

"Okay. But if you want to talk about anything—if there's anything we can do to help—"

"I don't need anybody's help." I recognize the hardness in her voice. It's just like Dad's.

"Misty, I saw the scars on your arm."

She pivots. There's panic in her eyes. "I did that a long time ago, okay? Not anymore. Don't tell anyone. Especially your parents. They'll just freak out and send me to a shrink. Or worse."

"Misty—" I don't know what to tell her. I don't know what I'm supposed to do. This is a mess. Misty is a mess.

"Promise you won't tell anyone, Rach. I swear, that's part of my old life."

I bite my lip. "Your life before must have been pretty bad."

The fear's gone from her face now. There's only anger left. "If you feel sorry for me, don't."

"But you had so much to deal with at once. Losing your mom, your friends, and starting in a new school . . ."

"I'm used to it. One year I went to five elementary schools. And my mom." She pauses. This is maybe only the second or third time, I think, she's mentioned her mom. "I lost her a long time before she died. It's all my friends I miss."

"You seem to be doing a good job making new friends," I say. Envy, anger, and awe are

26

peeking out from behind that sentence.

"I had so many friends up in Hibbing. You've got to get us there so you can meet all of them."

"Maybe Sarah can drive us sometime." Sarah's allowed to borrow her mom's car fairly often.

"Or I'll just ask Colt." She's so bold. She just met him!

"So . . . you and Colt?"

She laughs. "Not yet, not yet." She looks at me mischievously. "What about you, Rach? Do you have a Colt?"

I shrug.

"Dana and Sarah say you're into Kevin Liu."

I may need to have a talk with Dana and Sarah about sharing our secrets with Misty. "Yeah, well, I don't really have much time for dating . . ." I mutter.

"You study and stress too much. You need to have more fun. Your folks got any vodka?"

I ignore that. Mom's not drinking in front of Misty. "We'd better start studying now."

"I'm doing a'right." I've noticed that Misty, like Colt, tries to sound like she's ghetto.

I raise my eyebrows. "I heard your fight last night with my mom. She's right. You can get better than D's."

"Why bother? I'd rather have fun with my friends than study."

"You can do both, if you let me help you." I actually like the sound of that. I can help her. I can fix this. I can make things normal again.

"I just don't care about school like you and the rest of our friends." *Our* friends?

"But my parents do. Didn't Dad say he'd take the computer privileges away if your grades don't improve?"

"Maybe." Why is she fighting me on this? Can't she understand my parents are serious?

"I know you don't want to lose the computer or your phone. Right? So let me help."

She stares at me like a TV cop stares at a criminal. I break the stare by looking at her arms, but the long sleeves are pulled tight around the wrists. "Please, Misty."

"Okay." She bends to pick up her backpack. When she does, her T-shirt pulls up in the back.

And I steal a glimpse of red thong underwear.

8

"Misty, are you okay?" I'm just back from hanging out at Dana's house. Misty is facedown in the middle of the living room.

She lifts her head, but it drops, like her skull is too heavy. "I'm fine."

I drop my backpack and lean over her. A smell attacks my nose. Smoke and alcohol. "Misty, are you drunk?"

"I'm fine."

"What can I do?"

She pulls herself up to her knees. "Can you help me to my room?"

As I pull her up, I also pull up the sleeve on her right arm. It's a road map of fresh cuts. I pull, she follows, and she's upright. But it is only a second before she crashes again.

"Do you want coffee?" I've seen that on TV. I've never seen a drunk person in real life. She gets back to her knees and starts crawling like a helpless baby trying to reach its mother. Outside I hear a car—Dad's Lexus—pull into the driveway. The garage door opens. Crap. Dad *cannot* see this. "Hurry!"

I run ahead and open the door to her room. It'll take her forever to get there. I need to buy her some time. I pull out my phone and call Dad. He answers.

"Hey, Dad, I was just wondering, should we get takeout for dinner tonight? I thought we had more pasta in the pantry but we're actually out . . ."

"Rachel, I don't have time for this right now." He's short with me. Angry.

"What's wrong?" I ask him as I watch Misty's slow crawl continue.

"Misty punched a girl at school. We're

moving her to Rondo Alternative."

I do what I've never done before. I lie to Dad.

"That wasn't Misty's fault. I was there, I saw the whole thing. Shawna jumped her and—"

He grunts now and then as I spin the tale. Misty crawls a few more feet, stops, starts, stops.

"She's in her room now. She's upset. Let me talk with her before you tell her about Rondo." We make it to her room, but it's a struggle all the way. She dives inside and I shut the door. Seconds later, the front door opens, but Dad doesn't come toward us. We're safe, for now.

Misty's face down next to the bed. Denise's bed. Her bed. "Misty, what's going on?"

"I knew I was in trouble for punching that skank, so why not get messed up? Two for one." She laughs, coughs, laughs, groans. I hope she doesn't throw up.

"You know the first time I got drunk?" I think she asks. Her words are as blurry as her eyes.

"I was six. Mom was high, again. I was crying. She gave me vodka to shut me up."

I say nothing. I don't know this person and

her messed-up world and I don't want this in my life.

"First time I got high was at ten. Mom wanted to get high, but her regular dealer was locked up. So this other guy came over. I'd seen him before. He made her beg. He made me watch. Then he looked at me. Asked my age, but not my name. Then he said, 'Okay, let's party.'"

I think of parties at age ten. Cake. Candles. Balloons. Presents. Silly hats. Stupid games.

"So he gets my mom high, and me. You know, two for one." I can no longer breathe. "Then he says, 'Time to pay.' Mom sends me into another room so I don't have to see."

A minute ago I was worried Misty would throw up. Now I'm the one with a heaving stomach.

"I know how this goes down. I cover my ears, but I still hear it. Then my mom's shouting 'No, not her, not her.' Then crying."

"Misty, I'm so sorry," I choke out.

"The door opens and there's the guy. My mom's behind him, pulling on his arm so he won't come into the room. Her face is bloody, busted open."

I shout in my head but can't speak: *Don't say another word, please, Misty. Please.*

"He slams the door on her. Locks it." She says each word without emotion. "He says, 'Time to pay.'"

9

"So how do you think this happened?" I ask over lunch. We're all too wound up to eat. Kevin asked me to homecoming this morning. And Dana and Sarah just got asked by their crushes, Ed and Todd. "I mean I didn't think we'd be going, and then all of sudden . . . Wow."

Before the others can respond, my phone buzzes. Another text from Misty. Probably something about one of her new Rondo friends. She's always talking about Rondo people now, just like she used to talk about her friends in Hibbing. And she's always texting me during school, saying how much more fun she's having there than she ever did at Woodbury. I ignore the text and pick up where I left off with Sarah and Dana.

"What changed?" I ask. "Why do you think they finally asked us out?"

"Safety in numbers maybe?" answers Dana.

"No, I know Todd just couldn't resist my grace and beauty," says Sarah.

"Why does it matter?" Dana asks me.

"I just like to know things," I snap.

"Did Misty answer Nathan?" Sarah asks. Nathan was the odd man without a date in Kevin's group of friends, but like the rest of my circle, Misty's made friends with him online. She'd hinted maybe more.

"Yeah, she said yes." So even though she's kicked out of Woodbury High, Misty will be at our homecoming.

"Do you think your mom will even let Misty go?" Sarah asks.

"I don't know."

"Rachel, you don't seem to have much information," Dana says.

"Look, I'm not Misty's secretary. Why don't you ask her yourself since you're best pals?"

"Relax, Rachel," says Sarah.

"The point is we're going to homecoming and it's going to be great," Sarah says.

"So, we're still going dress shopping tomorrow, right?" asks Dana. "Should we invite Misty?"

"Are you *serious*?" I burst out.

"Rachel, you shouldn't be so hard on her," says Sarah. "She just wants us all to be friends. I think we should give her a chance."

No, *we* are three, not four. "I'm not being hard on her. I just get frustrated with her."

"She thinks that you hate her," Sarah mumbles.

"How do you know that?"

"She told me."

"I didn't realize the two of you were so close, Sarah. Maybe she can come live with you?"

"Rachel, will you just relax?" says Dana. "What is your problem?"

"My problem is that Misty seems to be taking control of my life! A month ago I had everything planned out, I knew exactly what to expect. Then Misty shows up, and suddenly there's all this drama at home, and now she's going to our homecoming, and *we're* going to homecoming . . ."

"Rachel, I don't know Misty that well, but she seems all right," says Dana. "And what does she have to do with the guys asking us to homecoming?"

"She knows I like Kevin," I say. "I'm afraid she told him he should ask me."

"So? You do like him. You should be excited," Dana says.

"What if I'm just his charity case? What if he just asked me because of Misty?"

"Rachel, relax," I'm told a third time. It's not a charm.

10

"You all look wonderful!" Mom snaps another photo of the four of us. Dad's all smiles. Mom too, for once. The boys are waiting, looking bored. The limo that Nathan's dad paid for has been parked outside for almost half an hour.

"Okay, boys, you get in the photo now," Mom says. She's having way more fun than I am tonight. Mostly I'm focused on resisting the urge to bite my nails.

The guys come toward us. Nathan stands on the outside of the group, waiting for Misty to join us. Mom relented and agreed to let her go. Even bought her a nice dress, though Misty hates it.

Now, Misty's door opens and she sweeps into the living room. Mom's eyes bulge. Though I don't look at the boys, I'm sure there are other bulges happening in the room. Misty's not wearing the dress Mom bought for her. This is from the Kardashian cleavage collection. At least her arms are hidden by black lacy sleeves. That's about the only thing that's hidden. And like her jewelry and makeup, this dress might as well have a neon price tag saying *shoplifted*.

"Oh my God, Misty," Sarah says, then giggles. Dana's not laughing. She looks nervous.

Mom's mouth stays open, but she can't seem to get any words out. I glance at Nathan. I'm surprised he's not drooling.

"Misty, go change," Dad whispers, though we all can hear. Like everything he and Mom say, it's code. Code for *We know you stole that. It's unacceptable. But we can't say so in front of our guests. So instead, you get this.*

"No," says Misty.

"If you want to go, you need to wear something different." Dad's tone turns a little tougher. "What's wrong with the dress your aunt Karen got you?"

"It's ugly!" Misty flings the word at everyone in the room. I suspect the real answer is, *It's sleeveless.* "But then you think I'm ugly, so that fits!"

"Misty, go to your room," says Mom. I know she wants to say *Leave this house* but can't. "You can wear the dress we bought you or you can stay home."

Misty pivots and seconds later a door slams hard.

"Okay, let's just finish the pictures." Mom keeps clicking away. Minutes pass. More photos, more giggles, and it all seems so silly, or am I just too serious?

Misty's door opens again. The sleeveless dress peaks out from under a huge gray hoodie. "Happy?" Misty says to Dad and then walks toward the group. Misty motions for Nathan to join her. He follows her like a puppy.

"I want you both home by midnight," Dad

says so stern that it almost makes me want to laugh.

"Okay," I say. Misty says nothing. She's too busy whispering in Nathan's ear.

"Midnight, Mr. Liu," Dad tells Kevin, then shakes his hand.

"Sure thing, Mr. Kelly," Kevin says, all man-to-man. He shoots a glance at me. I try to smile.

"Let's party! *Woot woot!*" Misty shouts as she leads the way toward the door. Hurricane Misty is gaining momentum. Tonight's set for a perfect storm.

11

"Rachel, honey, where is Misty?" I rub my eyes, then glance at the clock. 10:00 a.m.

"Like I told you last night, I don't know." Misty ditched us halfway through the dance. We left without her. "She's still not back?"

"No," says Dad, sounding tense and exhausted at the same time. "You're sure you don't have any idea where she might've gone after the dance?"

"Dad, I told you, I barely saw her once we got there." We'd actually had a great time at dinner before the dance, and we knew it was because of Misty: Misty's jokes, Misty's energy. For the first time, she felt like part of our group. Then, like she flipped a switch, she turned into party girl in the limo. It turned out she'd stashed both the scandalous dress and a bottle of vodka in the hoodie.

"Misty, put it away!" Nathan had shouted when she opened the bottle.

"Okay, I will!" She drank the vodka straight from the bottle. It burned my throat watching it.

Once we got to the dance, she hid the bottle behind some bushes and came inside with us. "Anybody seen Alix?" she had asked nobody in particular.

"Misty, do you want to—" Nathan had started, but then Misty bolted. She never turned around, and that was the last we saw of her.

"We need your help, Rachel," Mom says now.

Some help I've been so far. Everything I've tried to do to help Misty has blown up in my face.

"We don't know where to look," Dad adds.

"If you have any guesses about who she could be with . . ."

"Let me get dressed, okay?"

As soon as they leave, I boot up the computer and go to Misty's page. There's no clue as to where she is. I can only guess: Hibbing. I find the names of her best friends she's always talking about. Kylee, Samantha, Christy, Danielle. None have posted on her wall in a long, long time. I send each of them a message, asking if they know where Misty is, and I wait.

Dana and Sarah both pop online. I ask if they've heard anything about Misty.

SARAH TO ME: "She didn't take off with Nathan. Todd says he knows that much."

DANA TO ME: "I thought maybe she left with Colt, but I definitely saw him back with Shawna in the parking lot when we were leaving."

SARAH TO ME: "Misty was so out of control last night. I thought she was going to get us all arrested."

DANA TO ME: "Honestly, I'm glad she didn't stick around. It was hard to focus on anything else while she was there. And we still had fun after she left."

That's true. Kevin was his usual awkward but adorable self all night. I glance at my homecoming dress and think about the kiss he gave me when he dropped me off at the door at 11:55. It started out timid and uncomfortable, but we'd gotten the hang of it well before 11:58, when we actually said good night. For those few minutes, I'd been able to forget that as soon as I walked inside, my parents were going to freak out about Misty not being with me.

A new bubble pops up on my screen. Finally, one of Misty's Hibbing friends is responding to me.

KYLEE TO ME: "Who is this? I don't know you."

ME TO KYLEE: "I'm Misty McCullough's cousin. She lives with my family in Woodbury."

KYLEE TO ME: "So?"

ME TO KYLEE: "She's missing and I thought you might know where she is."

KYLEE TO ME: "Why?"

ME TO KYLEE: "She said you were one of her best friends in Hibbing."

KYLEE TO ME: "She told you that? That girl is whack."

ME TO KYLEE: "She talked about you all the time."

KYLEE TO ME: "Misty was just someone at school. I got no clue where she is."

ME TO KYLEE: "Do you think that Danielle or Christy would know?"

KYLEE TO ME: "Those are my friends, not hers. Misty was a locust."

ME TO KYLEE: "Huh?"

KYLEE TO ME: "She came in, took what she could from us, and moved to the next group."

ME TO KYLEE: "Well, do you know anyone who might know where she is?"

KYLEE TO ME: "Maybe she's visiting her dad in prison. He's at Oak Park Heights. Is that close?"

ME TO KYLEE: "I don't think she wants to see her father. She said she hated him."

KYLEE TO ME: "I never believed much Misty said. She told us her dad tried to kill her, but we looked it up. Turns out he's just in for drugs charges."

Before I type another word, it occurs to me that maybe Misty wasn't actually lying. Her father didn't try to murder her. He just helped kill her chances of living a stable, safe life.

12

"What answers did you get for number three?" Dana asks. But the only three that matters to me is that it is day three without Misty. Dad called the police after the twenty-four-hour mark. "Rachel, are you listening?" I look up, almost surprised to find myself in this coffee shop, bent over AP Chem homework. I've been reliving homecoming night in my head, searching for clues. "Sorry, just wondering about Misty."

"Well, can you try to focus?" asks Dana. "This test is a big part of our grade." Only a few days ago it was all Misty all the time. But the dance changed that. Sarah and Dana are finally ready to tune out the Misty train wreck. I wish I could too. I wish I knew how anymore.

"Todd's taking me out next weekend," Sarah says. "We might go bowling."

"Well, *I'm* not going anywhere if I fail this test, so can we please—" Dana starts but my phone rings.

"It's Misty," I tell the table. They go back to their books.

"Rach, can you get me?" Coughs. Clicking sound. Inhaling, then exhaling. Loud.

"Where are you?" I ask. More coughs, then a long pause.

"Um, I'm at the American Inn in South St. Paul by 494. You know it?"

"No." I know my little corner of Woodbury, that's enough for me. "But my dad could—"

"No, never mind. I'll figure out another way."

What other way? I think. *You have no real friends. Only ex-friends.* "One second." I look up at the others. "Sarah, could you drive me to get Misty?"

"Let me call Todd, maybe—"

"No, I don't want him involved." Not just in this, I think, but your life. Todd isn't part of *we*. "Please, Sarah, can't you just take us in your mom's car?" It got us to the coffee shop. It can get us to Misty.

Sarah sighs. "Fine."

"We'll come get you," I tell Misty, who coughs something that sounds like a thank-you and hangs up. We sweep our books into our backpacks, chuck our unfinished drinks in the trash.

Sarah drives us with directions on her phone. She speaks up as we get into South St. Paul. This is the hood compared to Woodbury.

"Rachel, I'm doing this for you, but I'm done with all Misty's drama," says Sarah. "It was funny at first, but now . . ."

Dana finishes. "Now it's just a waste of time."

I stare at my friends in disbelief. A week ago, I would've been relieved to hear them say this. But now? When Misty's in trouble? They're suddenly ready to drop her? To act like she doesn't even exist? Before I can find words to respond, we're there.

"What is Misty doing here?" Dana asks as we pull up in front of the run-down motel.

I text Misty. *What room?*

127.

I direct Sarah until we find the room. I get out and walk toward it. Misty stands in the open doorway, cigarette in hand. I look inside. Beer cans, pizza boxes. Filthy.

"Thanks for coming, Rach," Misty says. She hugs me tight like she'd never done before. We start toward the car, when I hear something from inside the room. A loud manly cough. I turn. In the room is an older guy with long hair, tattoos. No clothes. He winks at me. I turn away as fast as I can.

On the way to the car, I whisper, "Who was he?"

Misty yawns and then covers her eyes with her hand. "Honestly, Rach, I don't remember."

13

The reaction at home is predictable. After a wave of relief, the roll call of punishments.

"Misty, you can't do this to us, to yourself. Do you understand?" Dad asks. She nods. She's not saying anything to him, just like she stonewalled me in the car. She keeps quiet as Mom hands out the penalties: groundings, taking her phone, etc. Misty waits it out, then stomps upstairs without a word.

A few minutes later, I'm in my room, texting Kevin. As usual he's being sweet yet goofy, a little awkward but funny. He's a pinpoint of calm and sanity in the middle of Hurricane Misty.

Speak of the devil: Misty knocks on my door. I open it, invite her in. She sits on the floor. I stand. "I guess I messed up," she says.

"Disappearing like that? Yeah."

"I mean coming back here. I should've just told him to keep driving." I don't ask about the "him."

"You don't have to make this so hard for yourself. Just follow the rules."

Misty snorts, looks up at me, pushes her hair out of her eyes. "Easy for you to say, Rach."

"Look, okay, maybe I don't have as much fun as you, but I don't cause grief for everyone else."

"Do you think that's what I do? Cause people grief? You don't know anything about me."

I wish I had nails left to bite. I wish I hadn't opened the door to my room or this conversation.

"I'm not like you or your perfect friends." My perfect friends? Yeah. Sure. "I'm damaged goods. I know it."

"Don't talk that way about yourself."

Another snort. "That's how you talk about me, isn't it? Isn't it what everybody thinks?"

"That's not what everybody thinks," I lie.

"What do you think?"

I stay silent.

"I got nowhere to go. I can wait all day. But I bet you have stuff to do, Rach." As she moves away, she snatches my phone from my desk, and then stands in front of my door.

"Give me back my phone."

"Give me an answer." She leans against the door, a human barricade. "Just tell me the truth."

"Misty, look, we're different. Can we leave it at that?"

Misty walks past me, hands me my phone, and stands in front of my window facing the street. She opens the window and pushes out the screen. "What are you doing?" I say to her back.

She pulls out a cigarette from her purse. "I'm going out to hang with my Rondo friends."

"But aren't you grounded?" I ask as she starts crawling out the window.

"What are they going to do? You worry too much about all this stuff that doesn't matter."

Once she's outside, I ask even though I know better. "So what does matter, Misty?"

She doesn't say sex or booze or freedom but something much scarier. "Nothing."

14

"Are you going to school this morning?" I say to Misty's closed door.

There's no response. Same result when Mom and Dad tried earlier.

"I don't know how much more I can take," Mom confides in me. She's next to me, close. She's aged ten years in two months of Misty, who breaks every last straw she's handed.

"We just had *another* meeting with the Rondo staff barely two days ago," Mom adds in a whisper. "They've given Misty the benefit of the doubt at every turn. But she can't keep calling in sick. I promised them this was going to stop."

"Misty, people are worried about you," I say, mouth pressed against the door.

"Name one!" A shout comes through the door, almost knocking me backward. "Do you care about me, Rachel? Really?"

"Yes."

"Prove it."

"How?"

Pause. A noise, not tears, but something else? Razor on skin? "Tell *her* to go away." Mom hears, steps aside, and stomps off, probably to find Dad and discuss plan B or whatever.

"Misty, you'll be late." I push lightly on the door. It swings open and a toxic smell hits me. Every item in the room—Denise's dresser, desk, mirror, wall, all of it—covered. The room is marked with "x's" painted in various nail polish and lipstick hues.

"What did you do?" is all I can say.

"I made it mine." Misty grabs her nearly empty book bag from the lipstick-tagged carpet.

She doesn't grab her coat, but makes a bee-line for the garage.

As she leaves, Mom enters Denise's room. A room she helped decorate, organize, maintain. She says nothing as she surveys the damage, calculates the cost, and burns with rage.

"Mom, I'm sorry." Always, always, I'm the one who apologizes.

Mom turns and heads for her bedroom. The door slams.

"Rach, come on, let's go!" Misty yells from the living room.

I walk over to my parents' bedroom, press my ear to the door, and listen closely. There it is—a sound I'd never thought I'd hear. Mom's crying.

I put my hand over my mouth. Part of me wants to cry with her, for her. Part of me is oddly thrilled. Finally, a chink in the armor.

In the car, Dad's not talking. I could light a match and blow him up, easy. I'm glad he always drops me off first before taking Misty to Rondo. I wouldn't want to be around for the long ride into St. Paul.

I don't break the silence until I'm getting out of the car in front of Woodbury High. "Misty, why?" My voice comes out as a croak.

"Why what?"

"Why did you do that to Denise's room?"

She shrugs. "Why not?"

15

When I get home on the late bus after orchestra practice, I see an old, ugly blue car sitting in the driveway next to Dad's Lexus. "What's going on?" I ask as I walk in the door. Mom, Dad, and a stranger sit in the kitchen.

"We're waiting," Mom, Dad, and stranger woman say at the same time. I don't need to ask for whom.

"Sit down, please, Rachel. You should be part of this conversation," stranger woman says, so polite. "I'm Tasha Johnson, a social worker from Washington County. Has Misty talked with you about how she is doing at school?"

"Misty likes her friends and most teachers." To hear Misty tell it, she's Rondo's number one attraction.

"And what are her friends like?"

"I wouldn't know. Mom won't let her have them over here." Mom stiffens at my tone. This is as close to an act of defiance as she's heard. Dad looks at his watch, Mom stares at me, and I watch Tasha scribble into a blue notebook.

"Her grades are not good," Mom says. "She's fast on her way out even out of *that* school. The teachers have done everything they can. They've given her every possible chance. Nothing's worked."

"At Woodbury, how did she do?" asks Tasha.

They want me to give her up: tell them about Shawna, Colt, Nathan, the other burned bridges. "I didn't see her much. We had different classes."

"So Misty wasn't one of your homies?" Tasha tries to sound sixteen, twenty years ago.

"My friends and I, we're into different

things." That's true in more ways than one, I'm realizing.

"How about here at home?" Tasha asks. "How would you describe things for Misty here?"

I rest my hands on my knees. "It's hard for her."

"Hard for *her*?" Mom bursts out. Dad puts his hand on her shoulder. Tasha keeps scribbling.

"We're not what she's used to. We're kind of boring, and she's used to more excitement."

"Excitement! She creates chaos. She—"

For once, I talk over Mom. "Look, she's doing her best," I say. I readjust my glasses on my Pinocchio nose. "What's this about?" I ask Tasha, who does eye checks with my parents before she speaks.

"We're trying to decide if Misty might do better in another environment more suited for her."

"Another environment? You mean foster care?"

"Misty might need more structure than your family can provide," says Tasha.

"Misty just needs—" I stop when I realize I don't know the end of the sentence.

"She needs to learn to live in a stable family unit," Dad says. "She doesn't know how."

Mom sighs, looks at me like I'm wasting her time. "She's not learning that here, it's clear. Like now, she's late. She's supposed to come home after school. I set a rule, she breaks it."

"Maybe the bus was late," I snap. I've obeyed every rule and for what? Straight As, viola first chair, and four ulcers brewing.

Tasha starts talking foster care. Dad says nothing, not making the case for or against. At almost 5:00, just as Tasha's ready to leave, Misty barges in the door. She's not alone. Alix Hawkins is with her.

"What's going on?" Misty demands.

"You're not allowed to have friends over," Mom says, sharp. "And as usual, you're late."

"No, actually, I had my period on time this month, did you?" Misty says, sharper.

"You see, you see what I mean?" Mom whines like a two-year-old.

Misty looks at Tasha. "Let me guess. Social worker. You yanking me out of here?"

Tasha starts to speak, but Misty's already brushing past her. "I've been through this before. No big deal." I think, *It is a big deal, Misty. Save yourself. Say or do something before it's too late.*

Misty, with Alix behind, walks past us, down the hall. The steps stop and there's laughter.

"Where's my door?" Misty asks, more amused than angry. I follow the sound of her voice. And I see for myself: an empty doorway.

"She's shown that we can't trust her with privacy," I hear Mom saying to Tasha. "We're trying to show her that she needs to earn back that privilege . . ."

This definitely isn't Denise's room anymore. My sister wouldn't recognize it if she were here. Would she recognize anything, or anyone, in this house?

16

The slam of the front door means Misty and my parents are home, and boring viola practice is over.

"Do you have a maze you want me to run now?" Misty shouts as she stomps through the house.

My parents don't answer. I hear the back door open, another Misty-style slam. Mom's heels click on the floor. Fridge open. Ice in the glass. Then silence for an hour.

Until Misty barges back into the house and then into my room. "They think I'm crazy!"

She slams my door since she doesn't have one. "They took me to a shrink." Misty flops on my bed. It creaks with her weight and force.

"Look, they're just trying to help you." *We're all trying, but we don't know how.* I wonder if she's still cutting. I'm afraid to ask, more afraid of the answer.

"If I'm crazy, they can commit me. Lock me up."

"My parents wouldn't do that."

She laughs. "Rach, you got a lot to learn about adults. They need to show you they're always in control." I don't disagree with her. You can't argue with Misty because there's no logic in her world.

"They've got to get rid of me before Thanksgiving so Denise has a place to sleep," Misty says. Now that Denise's room is basically trashed, I do wonder where she'll stay.

"It's been nice knowing you." There's a seriousness in Misty's voice that scares me.

"What do you mean?"

"Look, I'm used to it. County took me away from Mom more than once."

"Where did you go?"

"Foster homes most times. Sometimes I ran and stayed with friends before they got me."

Another piece of Misty's life I've never known about. But my parents must've known. Must've known and chosen to do nothing, until Misty had no mom to be taken away from anymore, until there was no one else to be *responsible* for Misty.

"Why did they take you away?"

Misty laughs. "You're sounding like that head-shrinker."

"Sorry."

"Look, Rach, that's my life. I thought it might change. I guess not. I'm human garbage."

I swallow. "You're not, okay? Come on. Tell me how I can help."

She sighs. "Maybe you could help me with my homework. I've got this project for history class. I've been blowing it off so far, but the teacher seems okay. Most of the teachers there are pretty cool, actually, considering they're trying to teach a bunch of head cases. Anyway, I gotta try to do things right for a while."

I stand up, move toward the foot of my bed. "I'll help as much as I can."

Misty sits up, hugs me way too tight and for too long. "You won't regret it."

With her face so close to my nose, I smell alcohol and cigarettes, and know I already do.

17

"So Kevin finally asked me out—well, in—to hang out at his house," I say to Dana, all excited. Sarah doesn't sit with us at lunch anymore. She's all about Todd.

"Do you want to study this weekend or what?" Dana picks at her food.

"Did you hear what I said about Kevin?"

"Yeah, good for you, Rachel—you and Kevin, Sarah and Todd, Nathan and Misty." She pushes her tray away and pulls out her chemistry book.

"Nathan and Misty? She's good at keeping

secrets, but I've never seem them together since the dance."

"Oh, you didn't know about that?" Dana snaps. "I thought you were the information hub where everybody goes to get their Misty fix."

I put down my fork. I don't feel hungry. I feel like I'm being punched in the gut by Dana after Sarah already slapped us in the face. "Dana, what's with all this attitude?"

Dana opens her book. She won't even make eye contact with me. "Rachel, I'm sorry, but you're a mess. I can't deal with you right now, okay?" She takes a slow breath. "I think I need a friend break."

"A friend break," I whisper. "Just like that?"

She finally looks up, which is good, so she can see that I'm about to cry. "Just . . . for a while. It's just been different since Misty moved in with you. *You've* been different. It's too much to handle right now." She breaks my stare and fumbles with the pages of her chemistry book.

I'm not breathing. Maybe this was bound to happen, but it seems so sudden. It's one thing for Misty to destroy friendships she made two weeks before. But I would've thought something that's lasted this long, something that's always fit so well, would've been harder to break.

I reach across the table, rip the book from Dana's hands, and slam it shut. It's not the same satisfaction that Misty gets from slamming doors, but it's close. I leave my mess on the table behind me. Outside of the cafeteria, I find an empty hallway and break down in tears. I stop crying long enough to call Mom and tell her I've got cramps. She promises to pick me up as soon as she can.

◦ ◦ ◦

Mom pulls the car in the driveway, drops me off, and heads back to work. I trudge inside.

I walk toward Misty's room, pull the white sheet that acts as her door, but the room's empty. Then I hear it. Laughter. It's coming from the hall. No, wait, it's coming from my room. I open the door. In my bed, I see Misty on top of someone, grinding against him in just her bra. "Misty! Get out of my bed!"

"Crap!" She turns around but doesn't cover herself. "Uh, what's up, Rach?"

More laughter, but it's not Misty. It's from the person in the bed, *my bed*. "Hi, Rachel."

I swallow hard and pretend to look the other way as I mumble, "Hi, Alix."

18

"When are your parents getting home?" I ask Kevin. We sit together on the sofa in his basement. On the TV is an anime series we both liked as kids. It's only been a few minutes since he picked me up and brought me over. But he's not wasting any time. He keeps moving closer, putting his arms or hands behind me, around me, over me, against me.

"Later tonight," he says. "Sorry, Rachel, I don't know how I messed up. I thought they'd be here." He's a terrible liar. Like me, he's not the kind of person who messes up.

I cross my arms. "I don't think I'm supposed to be here without your parents around."

Kevin laughs nervously. "No worries. I'm a perfect gentleman." I shift in my seat. He uses that as an excuse to slide his hand over my left knee. "So what do you want to do until they get home? Watch TV or something more fun?"

Why is he asking me? He knows my answer. No. Not yet. "TV is fine."

"Cool. Let's change channels, though." When he reaches for the remote, he brushes against my breasts. "Oops." I have on a big sweater over a T-shirt over my A-cup bra. What does he think he felt?

A few minutes later he clicks the remote and turns the TV off. Clears his throat. "So. Want to have some fun? My folks won't be home for hours."

"Kevin, I'd rather just keep watching TV for now, okay?"

He sighs. "You know, Rachel, this isn't fair."

"What isn't fair?"

"We're going out, so what are you so hung up on?" Kevin says. "I mean, Nathan and Misty—"

"What about them?" His hand is back on my knee and creeping north.

"He doesn't want anyone to know they're dating." I don't respond since this is news to me, so I suspect it's not really dating. In addition to new stuff, Misty always seems to have cash as well.

"If that's what you're worried about, I wouldn't tell anybody anything we do," he whispers.

"There's nothing to tell," I say. "I think maybe I should—"

He makes his move: a kiss on the lips, a hand near my left breast, the other between my legs.

I make mine: a push away, feet on the ground, and sprint. Half a second later, I'm locked behind the bathroom door.

He knocks on it lightly. "Rachel? Come on, you don't need to freak out. Rachel?"

"Drive me home."

"Look, why don't you just come back out here and we'll sit and watch TV? All right? Come on, relax."

Relax relax relax.

"I want to go home." My voice shakes.

"I'm almost out of gas. I don't think I can get you that far."

More lying. How did this happen? How did I think that I knew him? He always seemed so perfect. So safe. "My parents can give you a ride when they get back. Let's just chill till then. Okay?"

"Maybe we shouldn't be going out," I mumble. "Maybe we should just go back to being friends."

"Just like you, Rachel—you never want to change anything," he snaps. "You've got a comfort zone the size of a closet." Or a bathroom, I think, in the part of my brain that can still think.

I say nothing. Minutes go by. I hear him sigh and trudge back to the couch. What would he do if I came out now and marched upstairs to the door? He wouldn't stop me. He wouldn't go that far.

At least I don't think he would. I wouldn't have thought anything like this would happen with him.

I look around. There's a tiny window on the outside wall of the bathroom. Tiny, yes, but so am I. I could climb out and . . . and what? Once I get outside, where would I go? How would I get home?

My stomach hurts and I'm sweating. I sit on the edge of the toilet. Scroll through the contacts in my phone. Dana. Sarah. The friends I thought I could always count on. I scroll through again. Then I see the name of the only person I could trust with this.

"Misty, I need your help," I whisper when she picks up. "Who do you know that has a car?"

She lists her "good friends" with cars, all Rondo people I've never met. Then she asks, "Why?"

"Hold on," I say, stalling. "I'll text you."

I hang up and pound out a typo-filled message with shaking hands. *At Kevin's. Need to leave NOW.* Then the address and the words *first-floor bathroom.*

Misty calls me two seconds after I send the text. "You stay right there. I'm coming to get you. Stay in that bathroom. That scumbag gets

anywhere near you, you kick him in the balls."
She hangs up before I've registered that her
words almost, almost, make me want to laugh.

In less time than I imagined, I hear tapping
on the window glass. I look out. It's Misty.

I open the window and crawl out, grabbing
Misty's outstretched arm for balance. "Thank
you," I gasp as my feet touch the ground. "My
pleasure," she says. Too loud, as always. "Let's
blow this joint." We break into a run.

I'm expecting an unfamiliar car to be waiting for us, someone from Rondo in the driver's
seat. But the car parked in front of Kevin's house
is my dad's Lexus. "You told my dad about—"

"I didn't tell anybody anything. I don't tell
friends' secrets." She holds up the spare car key
and beeps open the doors.

"So you just took my dad's car?" I ask.

Misty yanks open the driver's door and
laughs at the open sky. "I borrowed it."

19

Misty wants to know everything. She's this combination of curious yet totally self-centered. Still, I'm almost relieved when she demands the details. The story spills out of me before she's driven more than two blocks. When I'm done, she says, "Kevin Liu, who'd have thought?"

"Not me," I say, with a burst of air that's half-laugh, half-sob.

"We should go back. I haven't punched out a scumbag in a while."

"He's not a scumbag," I say. "He just—"

"Didn't know how to take no for an answer?

Yeah, I know the type." My mind flashes to ten-year-old Misty, the story she told me.

"I'm not ready, that's all. Like he said, I'm never ready for things to change. He's right about that . . ."

"Don't go there," snaps Misty. "Don't make this your fault. He's the one who was out of line. People take from you and they hurt you and then they blame you for it. They let you blame yourself. And it's crap. Don't ever blame yourself for things you can't control. This is not your fault!"

This is the strangest pep talk I've ever gotten. I wonder if anyone ever told Misty not to blame herself for everything she's gone through. I think of those scars on her wrists and can guess the answer.

We drive the rest of the way without talking.

As we turn onto my street, we can see that all the lights are on at the Kelly house. This should be fun.

By the time we pull in, my parents are both outside. "I had a fight with Kevin, and he wouldn't drive me," I explain as soon as we get out of the car.

"About what?" Mom demands.

"Stupid school stuff." My eyelids barely flutter when I lie anymore. Just like viola, practice makes perfect.

"Why didn't you call me?" Dad's turn.

"Because I didn't want to have this conversation," I say. Misty walks past us toward the house.

"But Misty?" Mom again. Misty doesn't turn. She's not walking, she's almost strutting.

"Misty doesn't *judge* me." I put a spin on the word *judge* that's a thing of beauty.

"When have we ever judged you about anything?" Dad asks. *All the time*, I don't answer.

Back to Mom. "We're calling Tasha in the morning. We told Misty that one more—"

"But Mom, she sneaked out of the house to help me. Doesn't that matter?"

"It's not just this, Rachel." Dad again. "She's having problems at Rondo. The staff has been in touch with us almost constantly. Teachers have given her plenty of one-on-one attention. But it isn't working."

"Isn't there another alternative school?" I ask. They don't make eye contact.

Dad leans closer and whispers. "Misty's going into a different kind of placement."

"Where she can get the help she needs," Mom whispers.

"Misty has more issues than we or Rondo can handle, so Tasha, your mom and—"

"And Misty gets no say in this? Nice. You're just another set of adults screwing her over."

Mom slaps me, for the first time ever. "You will not talk to us like that!" I absorb the blow, swallow my tears, and fix a hard stare on Mom, but I don't apologize.

"What was that about?" Misty shouts from the front door and runs back toward us.

"We need to talk," Mom says. I flash back to a day in August and those same four words.

"Rachel wanted me to come get her," Misty says. "It was wrong, I'm sorry, but deal with it."

"Rachel, could you go inside, please?" Mom's back to her polite fake self.

"No." Looks of surprise surround me. "Whatever happens, I want to be part of it."

Mom and Dad do the eyes-darting-back-and-forth thing. This is new territory for them. For all of us.

"Misty," Dad starts, "we realize you did this for a good reason, but that doesn't change the facts."

Mom finishes. "You were told you were out of chances. Actions have consequences, and—"

Misty finishes. "So you're putting me out on the street with the rest of the garbage?

Just because I borrowed your car to save your daughter from being raped?"

"What?" Mom and Dad stare at me and then back at Misty.

"Forget it!" shouts Misty before I can say anything. "You don't want me here anyway!" She pushes past us. Bolts for the Lexus.

"Misty, come back here right now!" Mom shouts after her.

"Misty!" I shout louder than Mom. She rescued me. I need to rescue her. "Misty, don't go!"

"So I borrowed your car, big deal." Misty flings open the driver's door. "Well, now I'm stealing it." Dad lunges forward, but he's not nearly quick enough.

"Misty, please!" I don't know why I'm still shouting. She isn't hearing me. "You're only making it worse for yourself!"

She's already backed out of the driveway when she rolls the window partway down and shouts back. "That's what I do best."

20

"It's called a seventy-two-hour hold," Mom explains over takeout Chinese.

As best we can figure, Misty drove Dad's car up to Hibbing and then maybe reality set in too deep. She'd run away but had nowhere to run to. Her friends had turned their backs, just like I had. And she had no backup plan.

My parents do, though. Mom spells it out to me as she fights with her chopsticks. "In Minnesota law, a person can be involuntarily admitted to a psychiatric—"

"You put Misty in a nut house because she

took your *car*?" I know the car's just an excuse. But aren't these the people who told me, just a few months ago, that we were going to make room in our lives for Misty? That they couldn't just abandon Dad's only niece? She was going to go Woodbury, I was going to tutor her, and everything was going to work out.

"First of all, it's not a nut house," Dad says now. "It's a regular hospital. She's undergoing a series of tests."

"Tests we should have had done before she moved into this house," Mom says.

Dad nods. "It's obvious that Misty's behavior is beyond her control. This evaluation will help us get to the root of what's going on with her. Then we can figure out what's best for her. Maybe a group home. Maybe foster care."

"Maybe *our* home." The words fly from my mouth like sparks. "Why can't she come back?"

Mom says nothing. Dad reaches across the table, puts his hand on mine. "I doubt that's going to happen."

Damaged goods, I remember her saying. Then I think of what she told me in the car. Aren't we all damaged goods, one way or another? "But if you knew what was wrong, then we could fix it. We could support her. We could—"

"It's more than that," Mom says. "We're also concerned about her effect on your behavior."

"*My* behavior?"

"Since she moved in, you've become disrespectful, made bad choices . . ."

"You've changed," Dad adds. "You're not the same person. We miss our little girl."

Their good, quiet little girl who had everything figured out. I miss her too. But I'm not sure she ever actually existed. Maybe the only real difference between Misty and me is that Misty doesn't bother pretending. "Well, I think people deserve a second chance. We're not all perfect like the two of you."

Dad grunts. "We're far from perfect, but we're trying to do what is best for everyone."

"Shouldn't Misty be able to decide for herself?"

"The problem with Misty is she doesn't know how to make good decisions," Mom says.

"And the problem with you two," I say, "is that you don't know how to deal with bad decisions. Including your own."

And for the first time in my life, I get up and walk away from them.

21

Nobody speaks as we approach the two-story brick building. It's been more than seventy-two hours, so Misty's been moved to a place called PrairieCare. "We're here to see Misty McCullough," Dad says to the tiny woman at a huge desk.

"ID, please." Mom and Dad hand her their licenses, sign in a book. The woman glares at me.

"I don't have any ID," I confess. "I'm their daughter."

"How old is she?" the woman asks my father.

"Eighteen," Mister Always Tell the Truth fibs. I sign in.

The woman speaks into a radio. Then she says, "You can meet her in room two. Through the metal detector, then to the right."

Like at the airport on our way to Florida fun, we pass through the detector. This is no vacation. Everything's washed out. Like the walls and floors had color, but something sucked it dry.

In a small room, we sit in silence on hard tan chairs at a tanner table. After a few minutes, the door opens. It's Misty, without make-up, and a woman in a uniform.

I stand up to hug her, like I didn't do when she left. "No PC," uniform lady says.

"Personal contact," Misty mumbles. "They speak their own language here."

I sit back down. Misty joins us at the table. She wears a large gray sweatshirt and sweatpants. I can see the old scars on her arm and the fresh ones, like the deep one on her left wrist. Her sneakers have no laces. There's no tie on the pants. She can't hurt herself here. Or be hurt.

"Misty, how are you feeling?" Mom says like she's talking to a tiny child.

Misty makes a fist with her right hand, relaxes it. After a deep breath, she says, "Better."

"That's good," Dad says. If this isn't the most awkward conversation in history, it at least cracks the top ten.

"So when can I get out of here?" She's looking at me, begging me for support, but I'm mute.

"That depends on lots of things," Dad starts. "We're meeting with the doctor and—"

"Why don't you just say it?" Another snap. "That you don't want me anymore."

Mom looks at Dad, who looks at the table. I look at Misty and I start to cry, for both of us.

○ ○ ○

I sit in the car while my parents talk to the psychiatrist. I don't know if Misty's part of the conversation. I wanted to stay longer with Misty, but they wouldn't leave me alone with her.

After an hour, my parents come out. No Misty, just a brown folder in Mom's hands.

"Where's Misty?" I ask.

"She's not coming home with us."

"Why not? They know what's wrong with her now, right? Can't we get her on medication—"

"Rachel, it's not that simple," Mom snaps.

"I don't need it to be *simple*. I just need you to tell me what's going on. What's wrong with her?"

"There are issues of patient confidentiality here," says Dad. "I'm sorry, honey, but we really shouldn't talk about it."

The drive home, like the trip out here, is silent.

◦ ◦ ◦

In the middle of the night, I creep downstairs into my parents' shared office. I find the hidden key to Mom's "family" filing cabinet. Open it. There's the brown folder.

It's easy to find because Mom keeps everything in order. Cabinet, house, life. Me.

I click the lamp over the desk, open the folder, and read the report with final exam-like focus. Under diagnosis it says: *borderline personality disorder (BPD).*

I read on. *BPD is a psychiatric disorder characterized by variability in actions, relations, and self-image.*

Below the definition is a checklist of symptoms. As I read it, each bullet point is a stab wound.

- Difficult and unstable relationships
- Poor self-image
- Intense but short episodes of anxiety or depression
- Difficulty controlling emotions or impulses
- Fear of being alone and abandonment
- Frequent displays of inappropriate anger
- Recurrent acts of crisis such as wrist cutting, overdosing, or self-mutilation
- Feelings of emptiness and boredom
- Impulsiveness with money, substance abuse, sexual relationships, binge eating, or shoplifting
- Periods of paranoia and loss of contact with reality

For each item, I flash to Misty. Like an action movie trailer, images come too fast to process. Fresh scars, red thong underwear, flask of vodka, stolen dress. I skim through the rest of the file, find the details about treatment. There's no magic pill or easy fix, though different medications can treat some symptoms, like depression. The recommended treatment is DBT: dialectical behavior therapy. I read the description. DBT is a long, slow process that demands patience and persistence. Definitely not Misty's strengths.

As I struggle to understand, I hear footsteps, a sigh, and the click of a light switch.

Dad stands by the door, looking defeated. "Do you have any questions?"

I let out a long shaky stream of air. "Just one question. When can we bring her home?"

22

"Do you think they'll let me have a door again anytime soon?" Misty asks.

The words get swallowed up by the still near emptiness of Misty's room. Dad moved the bed, a chair and the desk back in, but that's it so far. We sit on the floor.

"Sure," I say. "Just give it some time." We all need a little time.

"I haven't thanked you," she says.

"For what?"

"Convincing your folks to take me back."

I start to protest, to lie—to say we *all* wanted her back.

"Come on, Rach, I know it was all you."

I shut my mouth. After all those years of keeping promises to my parents, I've finally made a promise to myself. I'm going to accept the truth. Even if it's messy and ugly and out of control. And the truth is that my parents don't trust Misty. Don't really believe she belongs here. Don't really think that our family can handle her, that she can handle us. And I'm still not sure, deep down, if they're wrong.

Misty shows me her new stash of pills. "This is for the depression. This should help me sleep."

I nod, not sure what to say.

"Have you seen Alix at school?"

I nod again. "I told her what happened—that you were at PrairieCare. She seemed sad." I don't mention the rest of our conversation. I'd said, "I didn't know that Misty was gay. I thought, with her and Colt, her and Nathan . . ."

"To be honest," Alix said, "I don't think Misty knows what she is—gay, straight, bi. She's whatever you need her to be for whatever she wants at that time."

"What about your other friends?" I ask now. "At Rondo? Have you heard from anybody?"

"Rondo's taking me back," she says. I let the non-answer slide. "I promised my 'team' I'd study more. And I'll see a therapist on Monday and then go to a DBT group on Thursday nights."

"You won't have any time to get into trouble," I joke.

"I'll be just like you," she says, then laughs. There's edge to her statement, but I let it pass.

"I read up on Dialectical Behavioral Therapy," I tell her. "It looks hard. There's a lot to remember."

Misty climbs up on her bed, lies back, and says, "It's not like I have anything else to do."

"Well, that's not true," I correct her. "I can help you study, so you can get caught up."

"If you want to help me, I need to see Alix. Is there some way you could sneak her in?" she asks.

"I'll . . . see what I can do," I say, against my better judgment.

"That's not holding me accountable," Misty says, standing up. "Now I gotta put that on a diary card." The diary card is part of the DBT process for tracking emotions. I read as much as I could about it so I could help Misty through the process.

"Sorry." There I go again, apologizing. Old habits die hard. "Does anybody else read those? Your therapist?"

Misty shrugs and flops down on the bed. "Dunno. Shrinks are so weird. Who wants to hear about other people's problems?" *You*, I think, remembering Kevin. Like I can forget. Misty was there for me when I needed someone. Now I want to be there for her. "I mean, seriously," she says. "Who's gonna care about all I went through?"

I stand, go over toward the bed, place a hand on the end of it. "I do, Misty. I care."

Misty stares at the ceiling. "Thanks. When Alix gets here we'll drink to our friendship."

I laugh. A nervous laugh. But Misty doesn't join in. She's breathing deeply, relaxing.

"Before you sneak Alix into the house, tell

her to bring the goose," Misty whispers.

"The goose?"

"You know, vodka," Misty answers. "The top shelf stuff. It gets you messed up, no hangover."

"But what about the pills you're taking?" I ask, careful to keep most of the alarm out of my voice. "I'm pretty sure it's super dangerous to mix medication and alcohol." Thank you, AP Chem.

"Aw, Rach. You worry too much."

I stare down at Misty. She looks so calm. So close to being at peace. But I know her now. I used to think we were so different, but I was wrong. Misty is her own unique kind of messed up. So am I. So are Dana and Sarah and Kevin and my parents. Misty's way is just more out in the open than mine. Yet we could be twin sisters, under the flesh.

Words from this summer echo in my head like distant thunder—words that hold true for Misty as much as they ever did for me: *I don't like change.*

AUTHOR'S NOTE

One of the hardest parts about writing realistic fiction for teens is the desire to "make it real" while at the same time hearing from upset readers that the book didn't have a "happy ending." In some novels, I've sugarcoated, while in others, like this one, I opt for hard truth.

This is one story of one girl with borderline personality disorder (BPD). Misty might not make it, but many young women—and it is primarily girls who are diagnosed with BPD—do the hard work of therapy and come out on the other side. Others put in equal effort but still find their lives chaotic, and sometimes only aging seems to calm the fury.

The Diagnostic and Statistical Manual of Mental Disorders (DSM), published by the American Psychiatric Association, provides a common language and standard criteria for the classification of mental disorders. Before the publication of the 5th edition of the DSM in 2013, borderline personality disorder could not be diagnosed in people under the age of eighteen. Allowing this life-altering disorder to be treated earlier, most often through dialectical behavior therapy (DBT), may lead many young people to better outcomes.In addition to my own research, Nancy McLean reviewed the manuscript for accuracy of my portrayal of BPD. McLean is a licensed marriage and family therapist (MFT) with a graduate academic degree, clinical work experience, and successful passing of state-certified licensing exams. Along with a two- to three-year master's programs with a practicum and internship, MFTs are required to complete clinical training in individual or family therapy.

Finally, as with all the books in The Alternative series, students and teachers at South

Saint Paul Community Learning Center read and commented on the manuscript, in particular John Egelkrout, Mindy Haukedahl, Kathleen Johnson, and Lisa Seppelt.

ABOUT THE AUTHOR

Patrick Jones is the author of more than twenty novels for teens. He has also written two nonfiction books about combat sports, *The Main Event*, on professional wrestling, and *Ultimate Fighting*, on mixed martial arts. He has spoken to students at more than one hundred alternative schools, including residents of juvenile correctional facilities. Find him on the web at www.connectingya.com and on Twitter: @PatrickJonesYA.